Over in the Arctic

A polar baby animal counting book

By Marianne Berkes   Illustrated by Jill Dubin

DAWN PUBLICATIONS
CONNECTING CHILDREN AND NATURE

Over in the Arctic,
where the cold waters run,
lived a mother polar bear
and her little cub **one**.

"Roll," said the mother.
"I roll," said the **one**.
So they rolled on the ice
where the cold waters run.

Over in the Arctic,
hopping like they're kangaroos,
lived a mother Arctic hare
and her leverets **two**.

"Thump," said the mother.
"We thump," said the **two**.
So they thumped on the tundra,
hopping like they're kangaroos.

Over in the Arctic,
paddling in the icy sea,
lived an old mother walrus
and her little calves **three**.

"Kick," said the mother.
"We kick," said the **three**.
So they kicked with their flippers,
paddling in the icy sea.

Over in the Arctic,
curled up on a frosty floor,
lived a mother Arctic fox
and her little kits **four**.

"Hide," said the mother.
"We hide," said the **four**.
So they hid and they waited,
curled up on a frosty floor.

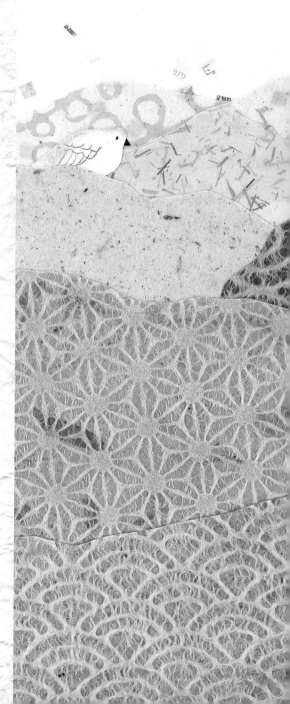

Over in the Arctic,
where they dip and they dive,
lived a white mother whale
and her little calves **five**.

"Click," said the mother.
"We click," said the **five**.
So they clicked and they whistled
where they dip and they dive.

Over in the Arctic
where the cold waters mix,
lived a furry mother seal
and her little pups **six**.

"Breathe," said the mother.
"We breathe," said the **six**.
So they came up for air
where the cold waters mix.

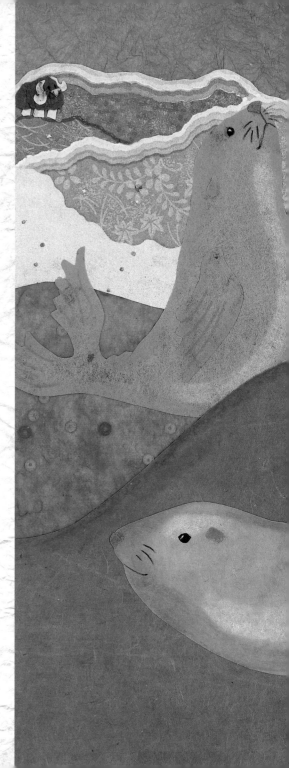

Over in the Arctic,
gliding up toward the heavens,
lived a mother snowy owl
and her little owlets **seven**.

"Swoop," said the mother.
"We swoop," said the **seven**.
So they swooped as they flew,
gliding up toward the heavens.

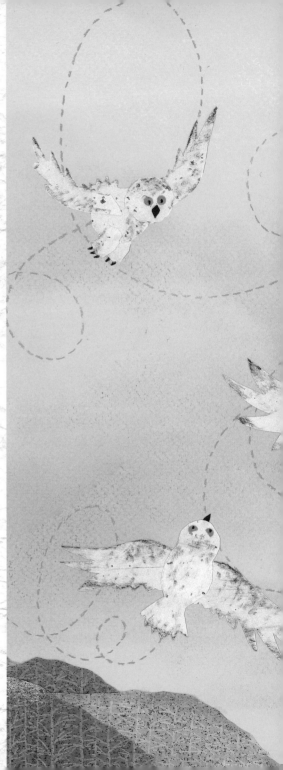

Over in the Arctic,
where some creatures migrate,
lived a mother snow goose
and her little goslings **eight**.

"Honk," said the mother.
"We honk," said the **eight**.
So they honked and flew south,
where some creatures migrate.

8

Over in the Arctic,
where the sun didn't shine,
lived a mother wolverine
and her little kits **nine**.

"Growl," said the mother.
"We growl," said the **nine**.
So they growled and they grumbled
where the sun didn't shine.

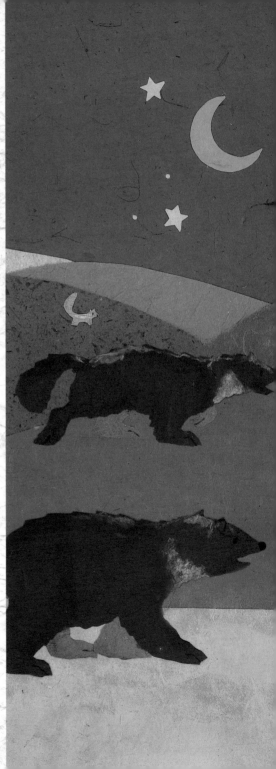

Over in the Arctic,
in a deep, dark den,
lived an old father wolf
and his little pups **ten**.

"Howl," said the father.
"We howl," said the **ten**.
So they howled in a pack
from their deep, dark den.

Over in the Arctic,
where the cold winds blow,
Arctic animals are living
in the water and the snow.

"Name us," say the animals,
"from ten to one."
Then go back and start over
'cause this rhyme isn't done.

Over in the Arctic,
you can "spy" with your eyes
to find more Arctic creatures—
every page has a surprise!

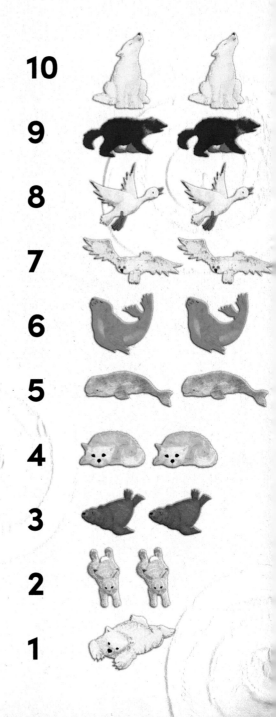

10

9

8

7

6

5

4

3

2

1

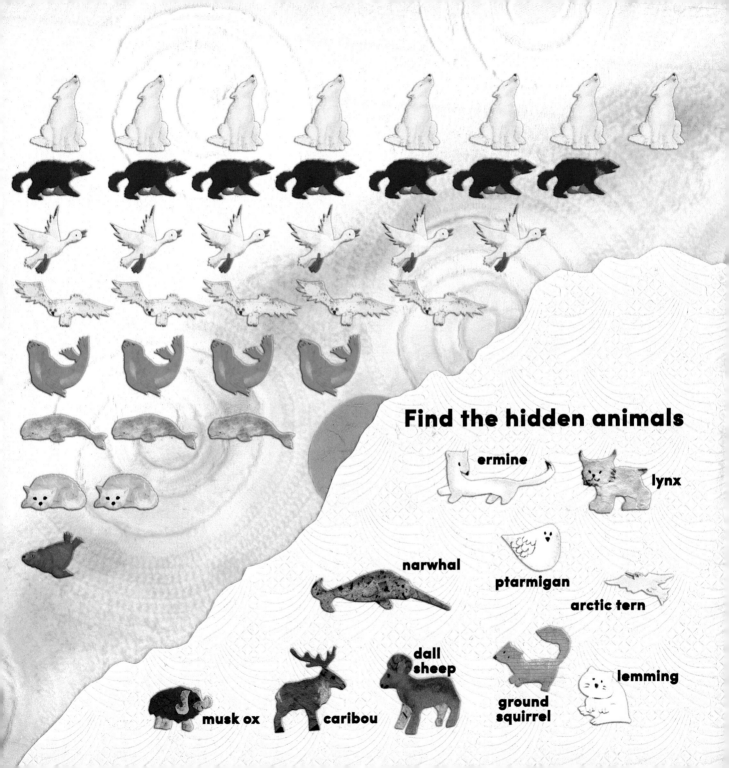

Find the hidden animals

ermine

lynx

narwhal

ptarmigan

arctic tern

dall sheep

ground squirrel

lemming

musk ox

caribou

Fact or Fiction?

In this variation of "Over in the Meadow," all the Arctic animals behave as they have been portrayed. Polar bears do roll, snowy owls swoop, and Arctic wolves howl. That's a fact! But do they have the number of babies as in this rhyme? No, that is fiction. While mother polar bears usually have one or two cubs, the Arctic wolf usually has four or five babies, and the Arctic fox can have as many as fourteen babies at one time.

Nature has very different ways of ensuring the survival of different species. The mother wolf nurses her pups, but when the pups are able to eat meat, the whole wolf pack helps feed the pups. A whole herd of walruses will come together to protect their babies from polar bears and killer whales. Both mother and father snowy owl watch over their owlets together. But a mother wolverine tends to her young entirely by herself.

What is the Arctic Tundra?

The Arctic tundra is a treeless plain. During the long, dark winter, it is covered with ice and snow. The ground is frozen all year long—this is called permafrost—and plants cannot sink roots into frozen ground. In summer, when the sun shines twenty-four hours a day, the snow and the top layer of soil thaw on top of the still-frozen lower layers, creating huge soggy marshes and lakes where dwarf plants can then grow. Melting ice and snow create many puddles where vast numbers of insect eggs hatch, which in turn attracts huge numbers of birds that come from faraway places to nest and raise their young. Whales also migrate as the icy Arctic Ocean warms up and swarms with sea life. But by October when the sun sets and doesn't rise again until February, winter returns and Arctic creatures must adapt once again to the harsh environment.

How do Arctic animals adapt to these extreme conditions? They have heavy fur and a thick layer of fat called blubber that protects them. Many Arctic land animals even have fur on the bottoms of their feet to help them walk in snow. Whales have blubber under their skin which keeps them warm even in icy water. Some Arctic animals have a coat that blends in with the color of their surroundings. This camouflage hides them from prey they are trying to catch, or from predators trying to catch them. Some animals hibernate, or go into a deep sleep, during the cold winter. Other animals go south, or migrate, to find warmer winter weather.

The "Hidden" Animals

Ermines are a type of weasel that are ferocious hunters with a keen sense of smell. Ermines have long bodies, which turn white in winter. Because they are slender, they can fit down into other burrowing animals' tunnels and hunt them down.

Lynxes are fierce cats related to bobcats. They live in Arctic forests near the tundra but not on the tundra itself. Lynxes have unusually large paws that act as snow shoes. They stalk their prey and can leap up to ten feet. Their powerful jaws and sharp teeth can kill prey with one bite.

Narwhals are toothed whales that live in the frigid Arctic Ocean. The male has a very long, white, twisted tusk on its head, so it is sometimes called a "unicorn whale." Narwhals have bluish-gray skin with white blotches and can grow to about sixteen feet long.

Ptarmigans are chicken-like birds with feathered feet to help them walk in snow. They can fly, but spend most of the time on the ground. The ptarmigan is the state bird of Alaska. It does not migrate but stays in the Arctic all year round.

Arctic terns are champion long-distance travelers! When they migrate, they fly over twenty thousand miles each year from the Arctic to Antarctic and back. The tern swoops down into the water to catch fish.

Musk oxen are large, horned animals with shaggy, long fur that hangs to the ground. They huddle together in herds and protect their young from predators by closing ranks. They are well-adapted to the cold Arctic environment.

Caribou are members of the deer family. They wander in large herds across the tundra. Related to reindeer, both males and females have antlers, but the males, or bulls, are larger. Males lose their antlers in the winter. They use their shovel-like hooves to shove snow out of the way to find food underneath, mostly lichen (a type of moss), sedges (grass-like plants), and small shrubs.

Dall sheep are wild sheep species that have curved horns and are closely related to goats. They have a furry coat that protects them from the cold. A rough pad on the bottom of their hooves helps them move well on uneven ground.

Arctic ground squirrels are plump rodents that live in colonies and hibernate during the winter. They eat constantly in spring and summer, and store food in their burrows so that when they wake up from their seven-month sleep they will have something to eat.

Lemmings are small rodents that look like hamsters with very thick, coarse fur. They build tunnels with many rooms in which they live during the winter. In the spring, they eat roots and berries, and gather seeds for winter. Lemmings are eaten by many animals, including the snowy owl and Arctic fox.

About the Animals

Polar bears have heavy, water-repellent fur with a thick layer of blubber underneath so they can swim in freezing water. They are often found on top of floating chunks of ice called ice floes and roll their bodies on the ice to cool down if they get too warm in the sun. Fur between their toes keeps them from slipping on ice and snow. At the onset of winter, the female digs an underground snow den where she gives birth to one or two cubs, and nurses them through the winter. In the spring, she teaches them to hunt for seals.

Arctic hares thump over the snow, racing away from predators with powerful hind legs. In winter, many hares huddle together to stay warm in a shelter they dig in the snow. Their brilliant white coat is an excellent camouflage. They dig through the snow to find and eat willow bark and mosses. In summer, they eat buds, berries, and leaves. Females give birth to two to eight babies, called leverets. Soon the leverets look like their parents and can breed the following year.

Walruses have large ivory tusks, which can sometimes be three feet long, and can be hooked into ice to pull their enormous bodies out of the water and onto ice. Walruses often weigh between two thousand and three thousand pounds. Walruses like to be together, and when not in the water, they huddle together to protect their babies from predators. When a walrus swims, it kicks its big back flippers and wriggles its whole body to push through the water. In the water, the calf often rides on its mother's back, holding on with front flippers. They dine on clams, worms, snails, and various animals found on the ocean floor.

Arctic foxes turn white in winter to match the snow. They curl their bushy tails around themselves like a blanket. Their tiny ears minimize heat loss. Fur on the bottom of their feet keeps frost out. Foxes eat meat, plants, and insects, often digging for food with sharp teeth and curved claws. When food is scarce, they hide near polar bears, waiting to eat the scraps the bears may leave behind. Females give birth to a large number of kits, up to fourteen in a litter.

Beluga whales are sometimes called "sea canaries" because they often "sing" loudly with clicks, clacks, squeaks, whistles and bell-like sounds. The "music" can last for hours. The sounds bounce off various objects and, like bats, they hear the echoes. This ability is called echolocation. The echoes enable them to know where things are underwater, including prey, without having to see them. Belugas are mammals and need to breathe. Echolocation helps them find small breathing holes when most of the sea is covered by ice. Beluga whales grow to about fifteen feet long and often migrate in large groups called pods. Females give birth to a single gray calf, which turns white as it matures.

Seals are related to walruses and sea lions. They have a layer of blubber beneath their skin which helps keep heat from leaving their bodies. Blubber serves as food storage also. Several different kinds of seals live in the Arctic, spending most of their lives in the icy water. As mammals, they must breathe, and because they can swim underwater for up to eight minutes, they have to make good use of air. When underwater, their heart rate slows down and they use their oxygen very efficiently. The mother seal gives birth on land or on floating ice to just one pup and nurses it until it is ready to swim.

Snowy owls glide over the tundra, scanning the landscape with keen eyesight. Suddenly they swoop down and catch prey while still in flight. Unlike many owls, the snowy owl has to hunt during the near-constant brightness in summer as well as the near-constant darkness of the long winter. Because there are no trees, their nests are on the ground. The female lays four to fifteen eggs. Both parents bring food to the owlets, who learn to fly at about nine weeks. The young owls, especially males, get whiter as they get older.

Snow geese migrate to the tundra to breed. They mate for life and produce two to six creamy white eggs in a shallow ground nest. The family remains together the first year, even though the goslings can swim and eat on their own within twenty-four hours after they hatch. When winter comes, the family joins a huge honking flock heading south. Snow geese are strong flyers. They often fly in a V-shaped formation; the goose in front reduces the wind resistance for those following. Flying in formation also reduces the risk of collision.

Wolverines are very strong, very aggressive, and have a deep growl. They look like small brown bears with cream colored markings, but are actually the largest member of the weasel family. Wolverines eat birds, eggs, fish, plants, roots, and fruit, as well as mammals. If they kill more food than they can eat, they spray the remainder with their musk (a stinky liquid produced in a special gland) and then store it underground. No other animal will be interested in the smelly food. In winter, the female gives birth to three or four kits which she tends by herself in a den dug into the snow.

Arctic wolves have good eyesight and hearing, and a keen sense of smell. They tolerate sub-zero temperatures, up to five months of darkness, and weeks without food. Their distinctive howl may signal the beginning and ending of a hunt, or be a warning to other wolf packs. The female gives birth in a den, usually to four or five pups. The male brings them food at first; later the whole pack shares the job, feeding them with regurgitated meat from a kill.

Tips from the Author

- Ten different verbs were used in the story to show how each animal behaves. Act them out as you read or sing the story.
- Ask: What were the ten parents called as babies?
- Discuss: Which creatures in this book migrate? Which ones stay in the Arctic all year?
- Compare ears, noses, tails, and toes of Arctic animals to some animals living in warm habitats.
- To find out how blubber keeps an animal warm, fill a ziplock sandwich bag half-full with shortening. Put another bag inside the bag of shortening, put your hand inside that bag, and squish the shortening around so your hand is surrounded by a layer of "blubber." Then carefully place your covered hand and a bare hand in a bowl of ice water. Feel the difference?

LET IT SNOW!

- On a winter walk, identify animal tracks.
- Fill spray bottles with water and drops of food coloring. Use the spray bottles to "paint" on the snow.
- Freeze some black construction paper so you have it ready for the next snowfall. Go outside and let some snowflakes fall on the frozen paper. Examine the snowflakes with a magnifying glass.
- Where it doesn't snow, make pretend snow pictures by mixing an equal amount of white glue and foam shaving cream in a plastic bowl. Use a small paintbrush or a Q-tip and make an Arctic snow picture on dark blue construction paper. When the picture has dried, the shaving cream will be puffy, just like real snow!

DISCOVER MORE IN BOOKS...

Animal Survivors of the Arctic by Barbara A. Somervill (Watts Library, 2004)

Arctic by Wayne Lynch (Cooper Square Publishing, 2007)

Arctic Lights, Arctic Nights by Debbie Miller (Bloomsbury, 2007)

Guide to Marine Mammals of Alaska by Kate Wynne and Pieter Folkens (Alaska Sea Grant College Program, 4th ed., 2013)

Tips from the Artist

The illustrations for this book were created using layers of cut paper. In my studio, I have a rainbow of decorative paper to choose from. There are papers that are solid colors and papers with textures that range from deeply embossed lines to delicate swirls. There are papers with all sorts of patterns like Japanese florals, bold dots, and intricate prints.

After researching the animals and their habitats, I make a detailed drawing of each illustration. Using a copy of my drawing as a pattern, I cut each piece out of decorative paper. Then I spread a very thin layer of glue to assemble the elements. Sometimes I use a toothpick to glue down small pieces. I then put the whole thing between two sheets of acetate and press it together under the heaviest books I have. This assures that each finished piece will lie flat. It's like putting a puzzle together! Each animal is made up of a variety of glued-together shapes. All the animals are glued to the background. I finish with colored pencils and pastels to add details, shading, and emphasis.

You can see a photo of the walrus art on my desk, along with a copy of my drawing that I used for a pattern. You can make a collage of your own. Although most of the paper I use comes from art supply stores, you can find interesting paper all around: in magazines, wrapping paper, or origami paper. Even the lines on notebook paper can be cut and rearranged to make interesting patterns. Look around for inspiration and use your imagination!

Making snowflakes is a fun and simple thing to do! Start with a square paper. Fold it in half diagonally. Fold it in half diagonally again. Once more, fold in half diagonally. Then cut out random shapes from the top and both sides. Open it to see your snowflake, tape ribbon to one of its points, and hang it up, perhaps in front of your window. As you make more snowflakes, make the cuts different and you will have lots of different designs. In nature, snowflakes all have six points. But it's difficult to make a six-pointed snowflake with folded paper. These are beautiful even though they have four points.

Over in the Arctic

Sung to the tune
"Over in the Meadow"

Traditional tune
Words by Marianne Berkes

O-ver in the Arc-tic, where the cold wa-ters run, lived a moth-er po-lar bear and her lit-tle cub one.

"Roll," said the mo-ther. "I roll," said the one. So they rolled on the ice where the cold wa-ters run.

2. Over in the Arctic, hopping like they're kangaroos,
   lived a mother Arctic hare and her leverets two.
   "Thump," said the mother. "We thump," said the two.
   So they thumped on the tundra, hopping like a kangaroo.

3. Over in the Arctic, paddling in the icy sea,
   lived an old mother walrus and her little calves three.
   "Kick," said the mother. "We kick," said the three.
   So they kicked with their flippers, paddling in the icy sea.

4. Over in the Arctic, curled up on a frosty floor,
   lived a mother Arctic fox and her little kits four.
   "Hide," said the mother. "We hide," said the four.
   So they hid and they waited, curled up on a frosty floor.

5. Over in the Arctic, where they dip and they dive,
   lived a white mother whale and her little calves five.
   "Click," said the mother. "We click," said the five.
   So they clicked and they whistled where they dip and they dive.

6. Over in the Arctic, where the cold waters mix,
   lived a furry mother seal and her little pups six.
   "Breathe," said the mother. "We breathe," said the six.
   So they came up for air where the cold waters mix.

7. Over in the Arctic, gliding up toward the heavens,
   lived a mother snowy owl and her little owlets seven.
   "Swoop," said the mother. "We swoop," said the seven.
   So they swooped as they flew, gliding up toward the heavens.

8. Over in the Arctic, where some creatures migrate,
   lived a mother snow goose and her little goslings eight.
   "Honk," said the mother. "We honk," said the eight.
   So they honked and flew south, where some creatures migrate.

9. Over in the Arctic, where the sun didn't shine,
   lived a mother wolverine and her little kits nine.
   "Growl," said the mother. "We growl," said the nine.
   So they growled and they grumbled where the sun didn't shine.

10. Over in the Arctic, in a deep, dark den,
    lived an old father wolf and his little pups ten.
    "Howl," said the father. "We howl," said the ten.
    So they howled in a pack from their deep, dark den.

Marianne Berkes has spent much of her life as an early childhood educator, children's theater director, and children's librarian. She is the award-winning author of over twenty-three interactive picture books that make learning fun. Her books, inspired by her love of nature, open kids' eyes to the magic found in our natural world. Marianne hopes young children will want to read each book again and again, each time learning something new and exciting. Her website is MarianneBerkes.com.

Jill Dubin's whimsical art has appeared in over thirty children's books. Her cut-paper illustrations reflect her interest in combining color, pattern, and texture. She grew up in Yonkers, New York, and graduated from Pratt Institute. She lives with her family in Cape Cod, including two dogs that do very little but with great enthusiasm. Visit her at JillDubin.com

**To the many children who touch my life. May you work together
to protect and preserve the wonder of the Arctic. Love —MB**

To Clark with love. —JD

**Special thanks to Mrs. Purdham and the teachers and students at Seminole Elementary
School for their help with the photo for the "Tips from the Author" page.**

**Thanks also to Mike Taras, Wildlife Education Specialist with the Alaska Department
of Fish and Game in Fairbanks, for his assistance with the manuscript.**

Thanks to Kathy Peters for her help with the photos for the "Tips from the Illustrator" page.

Text © 2008, 2021 by Marianne Berkes
Illustrations © 2008, 2021 by Jill Dubin
Cover and internal design © 2021 by Sourcebooks
Series design by Kelley Lanuto

Sourcebooks, Dawn Publications, and the colophon are registered trademarks of Sourcebooks.

Published by Dawn Publications, an imprint of Sourcebooks eXplore
P.O. Box 4410, Naperville, Illinois 60567–4410
(630)961- 3900
sourcebookskids.com

Originally published in 2008 in the United States by Dawn Publications.

Library of Congress Cataloging-in-Publication Data is on file with the publisher.

Source of Production: Wing King Tong Paper Products Co. Ltd., Shenzhen, Guangdong Province, China

Date of Production: February 2022
Run Number: 5025474

Printed and bound in China.
WKT 10 9 8 7 6 5 4 3 2

ALSO BY MARIANNE BERKES AND DAWN PUBLICATIONS

Baby on Board: How Animal Parents Carry their Young — These are some of the clever ways animals carry their babies!

Over in the Ocean — With unique and outstanding style, this book portrays a vivid community of marine creatures.

Over in the Jungle — As with *Ocean*, this book captures a rain forest teeming with remarkable animals.

Over in the Forest — Follow the tracks of forest animals, but watch out for the skunk!

Over in Australia — Australian animals are often unique, many with pouches for the babies. Such fun!

Over in a River — Beavers, manatees, and so many more animals help teach the geography and habitats of ten great North American rivers.

Over on a Mountain — Twenty cool animals, ten great mountain ranges, and seven continents, all in one story!

Over in the Grasslands — Come along on a safari! Lions, rhinos, and hippos introduce the African Savanna.

Over on the Farm — Welcome to the farm, where pigs roll, goats nibble, horses gallop, hens peck, and turkeys strut! Count, clap, and sing along.

Over on a Desert — Camels, tortoises, roadrunners, and jerboas help teach the habitat of the desert.

Going Around the Sun: Some Planetary Fun — Earth is part of a fascinating "family" of planets.

Going Home: The Mystery of Animal Migration — A book that is an introduction to animals that migrate.

Seashells by the Seashore — Kids discover, identify, and count twelve beautiful shells to give Grandma for her birthday.

The Swamp Where Gator Hides — Still as a log, only his watchful eyes can be seen.

What's in the Garden? — Good food doesn't begin on a store shelf in a box. It comes from a garden bursting with life!

OTHER NATURE BOOKS FROM DAWN PUBLICATIONS

Tall Tall Tree — Take a peek at some of the animals that make their home in a tall, tall tree—a magnificent coast redwood. Rhyming verses and a one-to-ten counting scheme made this a real page-turner.

Daytime Nighttime, All Through the Year — Delightful rhymes depict two animals for each month, one active during the day and one busy at night. See all the action!

Octopus Escapes Again! — Swim along with Octopus as she searches for food. Will she eat or be eaten? She outwits dangerous enemies by using a dazzling display of defenses.

Paddle, Perch, Climb: Bird Feet Are Neat — Become a bird detective as you meet the feet that help birds eat—so many different shapes, sizes, and ways to use them. It's time for lunch!

Dandelion Seed's Big Dream — A charming tale that follows a seed as it floats from the countryside to the city and encounters all sorts of obstacles and opportunities.

A Moon of My Own — An adventurous young girl journeys around the world accompanied by her faithful companion, the Moon. Wonder and beauty await you.